HOM

JEANNE WILLIS   PADDY DONNELLY

For David and Hermione Chambers – J.W.

For Owen, I hope you find a friend like Hom – P.D.

MORE BOOKS BY JEANNE WILLIS:

Daddy, Don't Let Go!

Not Just A Book

Susan Laughs

Tadpole's Promise

Dr Xargle's Book of Earth Families

Don't Go There!

Old Macdonald Had a Phone

Who's in the Loo?

The T-Rex Who Lost his Specs!

For a complete list of books by Jeanne Willis visit www.andersenpress.co.uk

COMING SOON FROM PADDY DONNELLY:

But Wolves, in Helicopters

This paperback edition first published in 2022 by Andersen Press Ltd.
First published in Great Britain in 2021 by Andersen Press Ltd.,
20 Vauxhall Bridge Road, London, SW1V 2SA, UK
Vijverlaan 48, 3062 HL Rotterdam, Nederland
Text copyright © Jeanne Willis 2021.
Illustration copyright © Paddy Donnelly 2021.
The rights of Jeanne Willis and Paddy Donnelly
to be identified as the author and illustrator
of this work have been asserted by
them in accordance with the Copyright, Designs and Patents Act, 1988.
All rights reserved. Printed and bound in China.
1 3 5 7 9 10 8 6 4 2
British Library Cataloguing in Publication Data available.
ISBN 978 1 78344 996 5

I've never told anyone about Hom.
No one knows he exists. Only me.
And you – because I trust you.

The grown-ups mustn't know about him.
They'll come and catch him and take him
away. But this is his home. He won't be
happy in their world. Hom is a peace-loving
creature. I don't know what kind
of a creature exactly.

It doesn't matter to me.
He's just Hom.

I met him after the shipwreck.
I swam to a deserted island,
far away.

Not one person came to
find me, but...

Hom did.

We'd never seen anything like each other. I'm not sure who was more scared – me or him! We laughed about that later.

He's hairier than me,

but not as tall.

I don't know how old he is.
It's not important.

We're much more
alike than different.

Hom is the last of his kind. He had a family once.
There are drawings of them in his cave.

What happened to them?
He could not say.
But I know he misses
them beyond words.

I often think about my own
family. Did they survive
the shipwreck?
I hope so.

I've drawn them on the cave
wall next to Hom's.

I wrote them a message, saying I'm safe.
I put it in a bottle and threw it out to sea.
Hom hugged me, like he knew how I felt.

We've learnt a lot
from each other. Hom
showed me which fruit is safe to eat.
Which is good, or I'd have starved.

There's no fresh water on the island.
I'd have died of thirst, but Hom fetched coconuts.
He cracked them open and I drank the milk.

He gave me his favourite stone.
It was shaped like an axe
and felt strangely familiar, like
I'd held it a million years ago.

Hom is better at running than me.
He can run for days...
and nights.

I love it when we go hunting.

But it was me
who taught
him how
to make
fire.

Hom was thrilled when
he saw his first flame.
I'll never forget
how his
eyes lit
up.

I gave him my toy car. He loved it. He'd never seen wheels before. He plays with it for hours.

Between us, we made a go-cart.

I fetched the driftwood, Hom did the chopping.
It was a bit wobbly but...

it worked!

We had so much fun but then I saw a rescue ship.

My heart sank. It was my chance to go home but...

I couldn't take Hom with me. And I couldn't bear to
leave him. If the sailors came ashore and saw him,
his life would never be the same. So...

...I hid with Hom until the sailors sailed away.

To this day, no one
knows I'm here.
Only you. But please
don't tell anyone
where I am...

or who I'm with. Hom is
the only one of his kind.
I must protect him.

I was the first person to see him
and I promised him that I will
be the last. Help me keep my
promise until I come home.

Then you can tell the whole world about Hom.
And when people ask what kind of creature he was,
you can put your hand on your heart and say...

...he was peace-loving, happy and free.